The Best Dad in the World

Melanie Joyce

Illustrated by

Steve Stone

igl+ books

I've got the **best** dad in the world, he means **everything** to me.

He's got a style all of his own and I'm sure that you'll agree.

My dad wears silly sweaters, they're **stretchy** and they're **swirly**.
He's got long arms and funny eyes and his hair is **strange** and **curly**.

My dad makes **brilliant** breakfasts, they're the ones I like the most.

His pancakes are **fantastic**, but he always burns the toast.

Mom says Dad can't cook, but I don't know what she means.

He makes the **best** plate ever of cheesy chilli beans.

I know I'm really lucky to have the **best** dad, ever.
He knows **everything** about the world and he's very, **very** clever.

When I'm all grown up, I hope that I'll be clever, too.

"You know so **much,**" I say to Dad, "I want to be **just** like you."

My dad is very patient, he says, "Don't worry, take your time."
I know I'm **really** lucky to have a dad like mine.

When I cry because I can't reach my bouncy ball,

my dad gives me a **hug** and says, "It's just because you're small."

When it's wet outside, Dad says, "We don't need the sun.
Put your coat and red boots on. The rain is lots of **fun.**"

When we're really wet, Dad says, "Let's go back inside.

We'll change our clothes and eat some cookies, by the fireside."

My dad spends time with me and we do **amazing** things.
He pushes me, **WHOOSH**, up to the clouds when I go on the swings.

Dad takes me to the theme park. We go on the **fastest** ride.

Whenever I'm scared, I know my dad will be right by my side.

Mom says that when Dad dances, he looks like he's in pain.
I think that it's **fantastic** and want Dad to dance again.

When Dad's special song comes on, he **jumps** out of his seat.
He **swings** his legs and **waves** his arms and **boogies** to the beat.

My dad is always fixing things. He really tries his best.

Mom just shakes her head and says, "I'm really **not** impressed."

Once, Mom got **really** cross when Dad repaired the light.

There was a **spark**, it all went **dark** and daytime turned to night.

My dad is a **great** pirate captain. **"Shiver me timbers!"** he booms.
I **squeal** when he makes me walk the plank and **run** around the room.

When Dad plays at Mr Underpants, it makes me **laugh** until I cry.

Not everybody likes it though, **especially** Auntie Di.

At night time when the moon comes out, we look up at the stars.

Dad says, "Let's pretend that we can **fly**, all the way up to Mars."

"We'll **ZOOM** across the galaxy, in a bright red, shiny rocket.

I'll collect some **sparkly** moon dust and put it in your pocket."

My dad makes up **spooky** stories and tells them late at night.

I hide under the covers, so Dad leaves on the light.

"Don't frighten him," says Mom and she soothes me with a cuddle.

Then me and Mom and Dad have a **lovely**, family snuggle.

When I go to sleep at night and settle down to rest,
I know that you'll be there, Dad. You're fantastic. **You're the best.**